ART, YOU'RE MAGIC!

Arthur Smith wants to be in the spotlight. But will he be a villain or a hero?

Sam McBratney's many books include the acclaimed picture book *Guess How Much I Love You* (shortlisted for the 1994 Kurt Maschler Award and the British Book Awards Illustrated Children's Book of the Year), which has sold well over twelve million copies

Books by the same author

Bert's Wonderful News
In Crack Willow Wood
Kristel Dimond, Timecop
Oliver Sundew, Tooth Fairy

For younger readers
The Dark at the Top of the Stairs
Guess How Much I Love You
Just One
Just You and Me

SAM McBRATNEY

ART YOU'RE MAGIC!

WALKER BOOKS

AND SUBSIDIARIES

LONDON • BOSTON • SYDNEY

To Oliver and Joe
T.B.

First published 1992 by
Walker Books Ltd, 87 Vauxhall Walk
London SE11 5HJ

This edition published 2002

2 4 6 8 10 9 7 5 3

Text © 1992 Sam McBratney
Illustrations © 1992, 2002 Tony Blundell

This book has been typeset in ITC Garamond

Printed and bound in Great Britain
by The Guernsey Press Co. Ltd

British Library Cataloguing in Publication Data:
a catalogue record for this book is
available from the British Library

ISBN 0-7445-8985-1

Contents

Chapter One

Mervyn Magee came to school in a new blue tie.

"I like your tie, Mervyn," everybody said. Even Henrietta Turtle said that she liked Mervyn's tie. Miss Ray, their teacher, said it looked like a lovely big butterfly.

I want a tie like
that, thought Art.

When Art came home from school he talked to his mother in the kitchen.

"Mummy, will you buy me a butterfly tie for round my neck, please? I want a red one."

At that moment his mother was helping Angela, Art's big sister, to whiten her gym shoes on the tiled floor.

"A butterfly tie?" she said. "What on earth is a butterfly tie?"

"He means a bow tie," said Angela. "He wants to look smart for Henrietta Turtle, don't you, Art?"

Angela knew perfectly well that Art didn't like Henrietta Turtle, but Art decided to ignore her.

"I think people would

"My sweet angel," said his mother, "everybody likes you as you are. People would adore you if you ran about in rags."

Angela rolled her eyes. "Lay off, Mum, you'll swell his head."

"Well, it's true. And of course you can have a butterfly tie. *If*," she added, "you promise to keep it good."

Art promised that he would keep it good. And so, when his dad came home that day he found three people waiting for him in the middle of the kitchen – and one of those people was wearing a brand new tie.

"Well, do you notice anything different?" said Mrs Smith.

"By Jove, that's some tie," said Mr Smith.

"Daddy, I picked this tie all by myself. If you want to wear it sometimes, I could lend it to you," shouted Art.

For some reason this made his family laugh. Art tramped cheerfully up the stairs to look at himself in the mirror again.

Chapter Two

Next morning, Art marched into the cloakroom with everybody else in Miss Ray's line. As soon as he took off his coat Henrietta Turtle spotted his new tie.

"Mervyn Magee had one of those ties first," she said, "and you are a copycat, Arthur Smith."

"You shut up," Art said.

Henrietta Turtle certainly wasn't
one of his friends and she never
would be.

"I won't shut up."

"You're not allowed to talk to me."

"I am allowed if it's true. Copycat!"

_____ me angry.

her now, __
zapping was
not allowed
in school,
so he said,
"Shut up,
Big Nose."

"Don't you call me Big Nose!"

Quite a few people had become interested in this battle of words in the cloakroom and Miss Ray was one of them.

"Henrietta Turtle and Arthur Smith, I want to see both of you in your seats right now."

Art went to his seat thinking how Henrietta Turtle should be moved into somebody else's class. She'd nearly got him into Trouble yet again.

After Miss Ray had taken the
register, the class practised for their
play. Art was a lion in the play.

Although he roared his loudest, Miss Ray did not say what a good lion he was and she did not say how nice his new tie was.

Art was disappointed and blamed Henrietta Turtle for this.

At break, Art's friend Katy asked him if he wanted to eat some of her yoghurt.

"I wouldn't give him any yoghurt if I was you, Katy," said Henrietta Turtle, "because he's a copycat. Mervyn Magee has a bow tie just like that and he had it first."

Zap, zap! thought Art. Boy, you

a big re

the blood out of your head.

Art was glad when Henrietta Turtle went away to talk to somebody else.

After break Miss Ray gave her class some number work to do. Everybody had to think hard, especially at Art's table, so there wasn't much noise for a while. Then there was a loud cry.

"Aaaaa! Look what he's done!

He's ruined my special giant rubber and it's my only one!"

Three quick-marching strides brought Miss Ray to the table where Art sat with Mervyn Magee, Katy and Henrietta Turtle. She picked up

Art sucked his top lip and looked down. Mervyn Magee smiled because he loved Trouble, and Katy chewed her pencil anxiously in case the blame should somehow settle on her.

"YOU DID IT, ARTHUR SMITH!" howled Henrietta Turtle.

It was true, he'd done it. Art's head hung low with shame as Miss Ray walked him to the blackboard with these awful words:

"Well, I didn't think I had any bad children in my class this year, but I was mistaken, wasn't I? You will stand there for five whole minutes, Arthur Smith, so that everybody can

see what happens to people who get up to silly nonsense."

And when they practised their play again, Miss Ray wouldn't let him be a lion. Art was not happy. When he got home he found his mother having tea with Katy's mum, who lived next door.

"Well, Art," said Katy's mum, "did you dazzle everybody with your new ... what do you call it?"

"Butterfly tie," said Mrs Smith.

Art was no fool, he saw them smiling at him. "I'm going to zap Henrietta Turtle," he cried, and his eyes were fierce and blue. "I'm going to zap her head off!"

That made the
mothers stop
smiling. Art
didn't care.
Up the stairs
he went to crawl under the bed and
lie there in the peace and quiet with
some of his toys.

Chapter Three

All the world seemed far away as Art lay curled up in the half-dark, thinking how this tie, the one round his neck, was a stupid tie. I don't want it any more, he decided.

A familiar sound reached his ears.

In the garden next door, Katy's
yappy dog was barking. Art began
to bark too, as if he understood
dog-talk.

And then a wonderful idea came
into his head and all of a sudden he
·⁓ ᵇⁱᶜ tie – the

⁓⁓

was lowest. Peanuts ɪᴏᴏᴋᴇᴅ ⁻ₚ
him, wagging his tail.

"Yappy dog," Art called quietly.

"Rrrrrruf!"

"I've got something for you here,"
said Art, climbing over the fence
into Katy's garden.

Yappy dog Peanuts had never seen a butterfly tie before and he didn't seem to want one – Art had some trouble fitting it round his neck.

At last the job was done, and what a difference that tie made to tatty old

Peanuts! Below the
straggly whiskers
that poked about
in the dirt all day
could now be
seen a splendid

~~d colour.

house.

And the butterfly tie
went with him!

Ding-dong! ding-dong!

Art heard the doorbell plainly from upstairs, where he sat in bed talking to some furry animals.

"Art. Arthur Smith! Come down those stairs at once."

Dad's voice! Was this Trouble? When Art went into the living-room he saw the red tie dangling from his dad's hand. It was dirty; it hung in tatters; it was all chewed up.

"Jeepers, Dad!" said Angela. "Is that the new tie?"

"It *was*," said Mr Smith.

"The twit must have been wearing it round his welly boot," cried Angela.

Don't you dare call me a twit,
thought Art. But he could see that
this was Trouble, all right.

"A little while ago," said Mr Smith,
"Katy's mum saw Peanuts the dog

down at the shops
with something
round his neck that
looked like a tie.
That can't be *Art's*
tie, she said to
herself, Art is
wearing his new
tie. But it *was* his
tie. She found it
later on the back
step. And here it is!"

scraty

"I thought it was his birthday,"
Art mumbled.

"NUTS!" cried Angela. "Dogs do
not have birthdays. One dog's day
is like any other, and they can't
count. There's something wrong
with your brain, Arthur Smith."

"You stop talking to me," said Art. But there was plenty of talking to be done and Mr Smith did most of it as he trailed Art back to bed. He was still talking about the price of clothes, and about the boys and

girls in the world who couldn't afford to buy food never mind new ties, as he tucked Art in for the night.

Mum came in to say night-night, and held up the lion's tail she'd made for him. "You'd better not forget this in the morning,"

I don't want to go to school and I don't want to be a lion and everybody's cross with me, thought Art. People blame me for everything. How many times had Miss Ray smiled at him all day? Not once. Art reached out an arm and dragged Big Bendy into bed with him, his true friend, and lay down to sleep. Was it true, he wondered, that dogs didn't have birthdays?

Chapter Four

Next morning Art went off to school
with his lion's tail carefully folded
up in his school bag.

   This was an important
Friday morning because Miss Ray's
class were putting on a play for the
other infant classes. Quite a few
mothers were coming to watch it
too, including Art's.

The play was a very good story –
Art was sure that people would
enjoy it. Once there was a bad king
and this bad king put Daniel into
the cave with lions. He thought the
͠ ͡ᴵᵃˡ but they

Daniel, and he was saiᴄ.

So, at ten past nine, the children
from the other classes came out of
their rooms and walked down to
the Hall. Here they sat in rows and
waited for Miss Ray's class to come
in and do their play.

45

The people in the Hall didn't know that there was a problem. Ernie wasn't here. He was at home in bed. Miss Ray had no Daniel!

"What am I going to *do*?" she said to Katy's mum, who was there to pin on Katy's angel wings. "How can I have a play about Daniel without a *Daniel*; why did he pick *this* Friday to get the chicken-pox?"

"Maybe you could do the play next week," said Katy's mum.

All the children began to groan.

Then Miss Ray felt someone prodding her with a lion's mask.

"I can be Daniel," said a voice – she looked down, and there was Art.

"Can you? Can you really? Do you know the words?"

"I know everybody's words," said Art.

"He does, Miss Ray," said Katy, "he knows everybody's words. He ̶a̶l̶l̶ ̶m̶e̶ when we were

There wasn't a moment to ̶l̶o̶̶ because everybody in the Hall was waiting. Katy's mum took off Art's tail and dressed him up in Daniel's clothes – a towel for his head and a stripy pyjama top.

Then all the lions and the bad
king and Daniel and the angel
hurried up the corridor as fast as
they could go.

Chapter Five

When Art got up on the stage in front of everybody that Friday morning he waved to his mum to make sure she knew he wasn't a lion any more.
And then the play began.

The best moment came when the bad king pushed Daniel among the lions, who walked round in a circle and began to roar. Art looked down at all the children who were watching, and he knew what they were

eaten.

Now it was time for Katy to say her words. She had to tell the lions to close their mouths and leave Daniel alone.

But she didn't. Katy couldn't. She was afraid to speak in front of all those people.

The lions were going wild! Henrietta Turtle, who was definitely the best lion, was roaring her head off and waving her mask about. The play was going to be ruined if Katy didn't speak!

Art walked across the stage and put an arm round her shoulder. "You'd better shut them up or Henrietta Turtle is going to eat me,"

he said. Katy looked at Henrietta and saw that this was true. She waved an arm in the air – a very angry angel. "Shut your mouth, Henrietta Turtle!" she called out. Her words worked like magic.

Henrietta Turtle closed her lips and sucked them into her mouth, as if she had no teeth. Then she stuck her hands under her armpits to show that her fierce paws didn't work, either. All the lions did the same and they looked like pet mice.

Everybody clapped and clapped.
Art's mum was one of those who
clapped the longest and he could
see that she'd forgotten all the
trouble caused by that stupid tie.

In the corridor Miss Ray swept Art off his feet and gave him quite a strong cuddle.

"Arthur Smith, you are magic," she said. "I have never seen a more wonderful Daniel and I think you're

More for you to enjoy!

- *Little Stupendo Flies High* Jon Blake   0-7445-5970-7

- *Captain Abdul's Pirate School* Colin McNaughton 0-7445-5242-7

- *The Ghost in Annie's Room* Philippa Pearce   0-7445-5993-6

- *Molly and the Beanstalk* Pippa Goodhart   0-7445-5981-2

- *Taking the Cat's Way Home* Jan Mark   0-7445-8268-7

- *The Finger-eater* Dick King-Smith   0-7445-8269-5

- *Care of Henry* Anne Fine   0-7445-8270-9

- *Cup Final Kid* Martin Waddell   0-7445-8297-0

- *Lady Long-legs* Jan Mark   0-7445-8296-2

- *Posh Watson* Gillian Cross   0-7445-8271-7

- *Impossible Parents* Brian Patten   0-7445-9022-1

- *Patrick's Perfect Pet* Annalena McAfee   0-7445-8911-8

- *Me and My Big Mouse* Simon Cheshire   0-7445-5982-0

- *No Tights for George!* June Crebbin   0-7445-5999-5

- *Big Head* Jean Ure   0-7445-8986-X

- *The Magic Boathouse* Sam Llewellyn   0-7445-8987-8

- *Easy Peasy* Sarah Hayes   0-7445-9043-4

- *Art, You're Magic!* Sam McBratney   0-7445-8985-1

All at £3.99